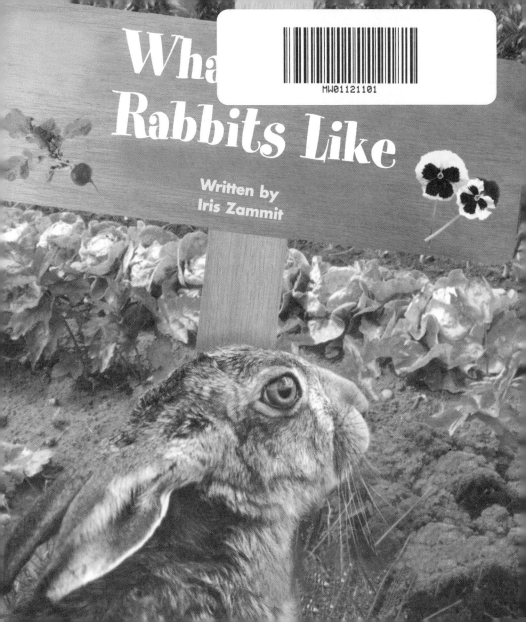

What Rabbits Like

Written by
Iris Zammit

A rabbit likes to eat lettuce.

A rabbit likes to eat spinach.

A rabbit likes to eat radishes.

A rabbit likes to eat carrots.

A rabbit likes to eat peas.

A rabbit likes to eat flowers.

A rabbit likes to eat!
What a fat rabbit!